Eeny Up Above

JANE YOLEN
illustrated by Kathryn Brown

Crocodile Books, USA

An imprint of Interlink Publishing Group, Inc.

www.interlinkbooks.com

First published in 2021 by

Crocodile Books
An imprint of Interlink Publishing Group, Inc.
46 Crosby Street, Northampton, Massachusetts 01060
www.interlinkbooks.com

Library of Congress Cataloging-in-Publication Data available:
978-1-62371-865-7

Printed and bound in Korea

For Michel and Hannah who have always encouraged writers,
and I am lucky to be one of theirs.—J. Y.

For Jane who with generous spirit took a chance on me,
and opened a door to my dreams.—K. B.

There were once three sisters who lived at the bottom of a deep, dark hole. Their names were Eeny, Meeny, and Miney Mole. In that hole dark was light, day was night, and summer and winter seemed the same.

The older sisters, Meeny and Miney, were happy in their hole. They loved the deep darkness of it, the soft dreaminess of it, the familiar tidiness of it. They did not ever want to leave.

But Eeny loved the world of Up Above. It was full of things both complicated and new.

She loved it in the summer, when flowers as numerous as stars dotted the green hills. She loved it in the autumn, when leaves floated down like flocks of silent, colorful birds. She loved it in the winter, when snowflakes like starshine tickled her nose.

But most of all she loved Up Above in the spring.

Meeny and Miney were not happy with Eeny's visits to Up Above. "Moles should be content in their holes," they told her.

"You could be eaten by an eagle Up Above," warned Meeny.

"You could be pounced on by a cat Up Above," warned Miney.

"You could be handled by a human Up Above," they said together.

Although none of them had ever seen one of these creatures before, the way they said the word "human" made Eeny certain that would be the worst fate of all.

Eeny asked her friend Worm what an eagle looked like.

"Eagle has a big beak and bigger wings," said Worm. "It likes early springs. And…" he shuddered from head to tail, which made him wriggle all over. "Best of all it likes early worms."

So whenever Eeny went Up Above with her digging shovel and pail, she was careful about beaks and wings, especially in an early spring.

Eeny asked her friend Centipede what a cat looked like.

"Cat has tickly whisklers and sharp claws and a long, long trail."

"As long as Snake's?" asked Eeny, for Snake was the longest creature she knew.

"Much, much longer," said Centipede. He shuddered from head to toe and all his feet tapped nervously on the floor.

So whenever Eeny went Up Above with her digging shovel and pail, she was careful about whisklers and claws and long, long trails.

Then Eeny asked her friend Snake about humans.

"Have you ever been handled by a human?" asked Eeny.

"I have nearly been hoed by one and almost tractored by another. I barely escaped being raked. But handled? Never," said Snake. "Humans don't handle snakes. Not if they know what is good for them."

"Can you teach me how to make humans afraid of handling *me*?" asked Eeny.

"That's a trick only snakes are allowed to know," Snake said. Then he smiled, all teeth and no lips, and slithered off.

So whenever Eeny went Up Above with her digging shovel and pail, she was careful to watch out for hoes (whatever those were) and tractors (whatever those were) and ever so careful of rakes (whatever those were). She looked out for beaks and claws, tickly whisklers and long trails. But she still had no idea what a human looked like.

One spring day when the light was sharp and new, Eeny went out to explore Up Above. Sitting on the ground near her hole was something she had never seen before. It smelled like the inside of a tree, where the heartwood is soft and inviting.

But the thing was not at all like a tree in other ways. It was short and square. It had no leaves and branches. It had no roots down into the soil.

Still, it smelled like a tree, so a tree it had to be. Eeny trusted her nose.

So she crept out to investigate, leaving her home underground far behind.

Around one side of the short, square, leafless tree was a hole just her size. At that moment the ground behind her began to shake, little trembles like water running down.

Then the trembles got bigger and closer.

Is it a hoe? Eeny wondered.

Is it a tractor? Eeny worried.

Is it a rake?

She remembered what Snake had told her. She remembered Snake's peculiar smile. The trembles got nearer still.

Eeny's heart was going pitter-pitter-pat so fast she could feel it in her throat and in her nose. She could feel it in her tummy and in her teeth. Without thinking, she jumped right into the hole in the short, square tree, forgetting her shovel and her pail outside.

It was dark inside the hole, but that was all right. Eeny liked the dark. Dark was warm and soft and tucked around her like a blanket. Dark was familiar and safe. She settled down in the dark to wait till the trembling ground got quiet and the danger went far, far away.

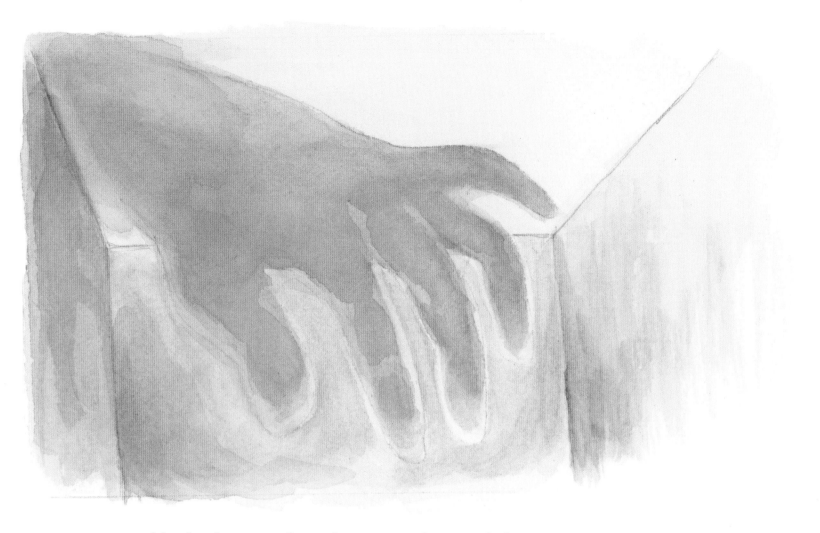

But suddenly the tree above her opened up and the spring light poured down, hard as hail. Something large with five wriggly parts, each pink as new roots, came down over her head.

The Something was not sharp like beaks or claws. It was not tickly like whisklers. It was not long like a trail.

The Something smelled of dirt and digging. It smelled of flowers and potato buds and corn. It smelled complicated and new.

Complicated and new!

Eeny suddenly remembered that she loved complicated and new, the way her sisters loved familiar and safe. "*Some* moles," she reminded herself, "are content in their old holes. But *some* moles are not me!"

She turned her face up to the Something. She gave what she thought was a smile like Snake's, though it was not nearly as wide as his.

The Something picked her up and carried her high in the air till she saw an eye as big as her body. The eye was the color of the ground in the spring. Eeny realized that the eye and the paw were parts of the same Something. And the paw connected to a body, and the body to legs, and—well, it was better not to think about how big the entire Something was.

Then there came a voice like grumbly thunder. "Aren't you a teeny little mole."

"Not teeny—Eeny," said Eeny. But her voice was tiny and squeaked.

They stared at each other for a long, long time. Eeny sniffed the Something's paw, and the Something's paw stroked the back of Eeny's neck. The feeling was soft and comforting and new, like spring.

Then the Something carried Eeny through the air, so carefully she was never afraid, and placed her tenderly on the ground.

When Eeny realized she was right by her very own hole, she looked up.

And up.

And up.

She knew then that the Something was not an eagle, for it had no beak or claws. She knew that it was not a cat, for it had no whisklers or trail.

She knew that the Something was a human.

She waved her little paw at the human, and it waved its big, wriggly pink paw back at her.

Then Eeny jumped into her very own hole.

"Wait, little mole! You've forgotten something!"

Her shovel and pail came scootling down after her.

Eeny picked them up. "I shall have to tell Meeny and Miney that I have been handled! And it was not scary at all. In fact it was a rather nice sort of feeling, not a bit like being pounced on or eaten. Won't they be surprised!"

And she ran off down the hole into the warm, familiar dark of home.